Andy Barrett, you know how to snat
chest.

The writing, as always, is crisp, immediate and loaded with sarcasm.

This book is dark and ugly but has just enough humour dotted around to make you giggle when you know you really shouldn't.

This novella sucks you right in from the first page.

Barrett is the master of tension with laugh out loud moments interspersed throughout.

I had to remind myself to breathe. The Lock is graphic, imaginative, and brilliantly written. Truly breath-taking.

I love how the tension escalates.

Try to stop reading....you can't!

Andrew Barrett is a master of his game!

"The Lock" by Andrew Barrett is a macabre little thriller of a novella.

With the class of Alfred Hitchcock, a seriously disturbing black and white story that will keep you awake after you hit the sack.

This is my favourite Eddie Collins CSI novella yet!

I love the way Andrew Barrett adds the wit and humour into the story.

Brilliant story, great humour and very scary! Loved It!

This is the first Andrew Barrett short story since the phenomenal "The Note" It does not disappoint!

This is a spine-tingling tale which will take you to a place you will never want to revisit.

Chores did not get completed today but this book got read!

Walk with Eddie as Andrew Barrett takes you on another exploration of the human condition armed with nothing more than Eddie's dark wit.

The suspense, humour and plot twists will keep you reading to the last page.

I went from my heart feeling like it was going to come out of my chest due to the tense circumstances, to laughing very loudly at Eddie's inappropriate wit.

Andrew Barrett is fast becoming one of my favorite authors.

This is a novella-size read but full of reading.

This is a sit on the edge of your seat, scary book. It draws you in page by page. Very cleverly written.

This was a fun read. The ending was great, Eddie was Eddie.

Good luck with any efforts to not read this in one sitting. I took a break, but only because one has to eat.

The story is gripping and horrific at the same time.

Loving the inappropriate humour of the main character.

A horror story, some really gruesome details and descriptions. You don't see it coming, it just hits you up the face.

Andrew Barrett writes some of the best thrillers around.

Wow! This book was very intense. Sometimes I noticed I was holding my breath while reading it.

Had me scared out of my wits one minute laughing myself silly the next!

Oh how I love Andy's writing!

This book is dark and twisted; it will make the hairs on the back of your neck stand on end.

Although this book is a novella it packs a mighty punch and will keep you hooked.

THE LOCK

A CSI Eddie Collins Novella

by

Andrew Barrett

Gemma,

Hope you enjoy your copy of
the Lock,

Take care,

Andy Barrett

Jan/9

PART ONE

Through the crack in the door I watched as they made their way into the room by torchlight, amazed by what they'd found. Their eyes were wide; they were frightened, and for good reason. I smiled and watched them go in deeper to where the machines were.

The Key

When I arrived at work this morning, I couldn't wait to go home. I love my job – I know how hard that might be to believe, but I really do. It's the office parts of my job that weigh so heavily in the pit of my stomach that I feel it growing a new ulcer each and every day. Those, and the politics, and the lack of staff and resources.

They like change in the police force. I don't. I like to get used to the way something works or the way we do things, and become really good at using it or doing it, whereas the bosses seem ill-at-ease with being good at anything – and consequently are shit at everything. We're perpetually learning new things, getting used to them, and finding string-and-sticky-tape solutions when they break, which is usually every bastard day.

If it ain't broke, don't fix it.

If it is broke, pretend it's not.

And they wonder why we're never at our best. I live in a state of perpetual perplexity at their incompetence. They change things for the sake of it, and that just makes my life a miserable version of hell. And the more I kick back against it, the more I'm labelled Not Good With Change. My boss said I was intimidating. I stared at him until he apologised.

I don't care, really; that label, and others like it, keep people away from me, and so I don't have to put up with their bullshit all that often. What I do have to put up with is being sent to jobs that no one else wants.

This job is a suspected abduction of a fifteen-year-old boy. Really? A suspected abduction? He's off somewhere discovering the delights of the female of the species while he's off the radar. I'd engage in that kind of thing too if it didn't mean twenty minutes of small-talk before we got down to the bump and grind, followed by another twenty minutes of apologising. But who can be bothered?

The boy was last seen leaving school with his mates, and then he veered off and went ahead alone, aiming for a stretch of woodland between the school and a local industrial estate. Romantic, huh?

Okay, I admit that my earlier comments were premature, maybe a bit cynical. Someone found his school bag.

The contents were emptied across the decaying fallen leaves and the mud, pages of exercise books whipping back and forth in the wind as they became trapped against trees and in the bracken. Pens and pencils, other items of colourful stationery strewn across the woodland floor, glistened in a brief outing of sunlight.

Honestly, it's a wonder I don't have fucking rickets, living in Leeds in the autumn – there's barely enough sunlight to see the switch on your torch.

Anyway, I stood at the periphery of the scene, growing colder, my nose getting redder, my fingers getting number, discussing the finer points of the investigation with a Detective Constable who was hugging himself against the wind, and who had given up looking at me a long time ago, and was now just nodding, pretending to care. A dew drop dangled under the tip of his nose.

"Who secured the scene?" I asked, fascinated, waiting for it to be blown away.

He shrugged, and said, "Ask him." His index finger protruded from beneath an arm, pointing at a Police Community Support Officer who was shivering ten or twelve yards away, hopping from foot to foot as though he was about to piss his pants. "He might know."

I looked at the PCSO. He looked at me. I could tell he wasn't up for a conversation, so I just forgot all about it, and entered the scene. All I was concerned with was retrieving the boy's belongings without destroying anything that might be on them. Surprised? Well, when you have no story to go on, you just try and cover the bases, and when it later becomes clear what's happened, you can devise a plan based on whatever evidence you've got. If the kid showed up with a big smile on his face, then great; give him his gear back, wink at him, and send him on his way with a leaflet about safe sex.

If he turned up dead, then you might want to consider having all those school books looked at for fingerprints after they'd been treated with ninhydrin. We might catch us a killer just as easily as that. You get my meaning, though. I looked at the papers, at the books whose pages reminded me of a delicate Japanese fan as the wind rippled through them backward and forward, and all I could see, obliterating the atrocious handwriting, were one or two footwear marks. There were more in the soft mud nearby.

They were copper's boots. Recognise them a mile away. I drew in a breath through my nose until it felt like both nostrils had iced up. The incompetent bastards, cordoning off a scene to preserve it and then trampling half the fucking evidence. Yes, it was cold, and no one wanted to be here being bitten by a wind with pins for teeth, but I expected higher standards.

It was as I was considering what to do that the inevitable happened.

"Bravo-Seven-Two?"

I closed my eyes and felt my nose begin to run. I dragged a sleeve across it and answered, full of enthusiasm. "Go ahead."

"Bravo-Seven-Two, sorry to disturb you, but Division are enquiring how long you're going to be; they have a sudden death they'd like you to attend."

My first instinct was to smash the fucking radio to bits.

They don't like it when you do that. I've had one or two meetings about it. They also don't like it when you just take the battery off the radio and pretend you didn't hear them. Had meetings about that too.

My second reaction was *how fucking dare you line up another job for me when I haven't even finished this bastard yet? Isn't anyone else working today? Jesus!*

And then I had a third reaction: I wondered if it was an indoor scene. Somewhere warm. And I really don't mind dead people – so long as they're reasonably fresh.

I looked at the school books, at the bag that had been turned upside down and thrown unto the undergrowth. I looked at DC Icicle and the Glaring PCSO.

"Bravo-Seven-Two: give me twenty minutes here and I'll be en route."

* * *

Less than an hour later I was toasty warm. This job here is a sudden death – a favourite of mine because the client doesn't often talk back.

This particular client was an old man. His face looked as though it was made for a head twice as big as the one he had. It hung off him in folds and creases that you could trip over if you didn't watch where you were going. His skin was white. Not just pale; fucking white. Put him on stage as Dracula and he wouldn't need any makeup.

"Now there's a case for vitamin D," I said to myself. Perhaps I was being too harsh – death never made anyone look better. Well, almost never.

He was found on his bedroom floor by his regular carer.

Poor man, I thought, as I walked around his room taking photographs to show how precisely neat and tidy it was. Well, neat and tidy if you didn't include the dead body in the middle of the floor. I felt sure he'd rather have died in bed given the mess a leaking body can produce. The copper on scene guard duty told me the old guy was called Albert Crabtree, and he was eighty-two years old. He knew this because the carer had told him.

And, as his name suggested, he was a crabby old bastard, and the carer was glad to get him off her books. Some people look content in death, but he still looked like a crabby old bastard, and I'd bet he'd order her to clean up his shit pronto if he could. And get rid of them blasted flies, woman! The carer had gone on to say that she was worried about the other brother, Frederick – hadn't seen him in ages, and each time she'd asked after him, Albert had ignored her.

I smiled at him, and at the lower denture that had popped out of his slack mouth, and the dimples either side of his nose where his spectacles had lived. And I gawped at his décor. Faded patterned paper somehow still clung to his bedroom walls sixty years after he'd first hung it. And the sepia-toned photos in plain wooden frames were genuine sepia and not the product of photographic software. Suddenly I liked this guy! The holes in the linoleum floor had worn smooth at the edges and the dirt in the exposed floorboards beneath was shiny, as were the tack heads holding those smooth edges down – that was Albert's version of a good health and safety policy.

He didn't believe in change for change's sake.

On the proper wooden bedside table, the one with brass loop handles on the two drawers, stood a Westclox alarm clock from the sixties. It was still going, and it didn't take too much imagination to see that Albert had seen no reason to bin it in favour of the characterless plastic shit they sold these days. The clock still worked: leave it alone, and save your cash. Yep, I think I would have got along okay with Albert Crabtree. He could have taught my bosses a thing or two.

As it turned out, Albert, the old stalwart, succumbed to that thing that gets us all in the end: death. And he didn't look too happy about it either, as though he had urgent unfinished business to attend to. I wondered why he'd croaked.

He was in the middle of his bedroom floor. He was fully clothed. He died somewhere between ten yesterday morning and four this afternoon. I bent and took hold of his cardigan sleeve. His arm lifted easily enough and that told me he'd been dead over twenty-four hours. Not that it had much bearing on things.

This old detached thing was built of stone, and stood proudly in an acre of woodland and grassland, and I thought it matched the owner well: secluded yet pretentious. Having said that, old Albert didn't look pretentious right now, granted. It was half a mile from the medieval ruins of Kirkstall Abbey. It was easy to tell that Albert had tried his best to keep up the place by himself, but at eighty-two, you're not going to be trimming the conifers too often or cutting the lawns and sorting out the shrubbery. I bet he had groundsmen for that kind of thing – even if they were the kind who only came weekly for a couple of hours.

If you nailed me down, I'd say the house looked like an old vicarage: dark stone gables, pointy towers, thick walls, and large windows in each high-ceilinged room. I suspect it would have had a kitchen downstairs in the cellar. It looked like a house owned by someone rich enough to have employed staff in Victorian days, and I planned on having a little scout round soon to satisfy my curiosity that nothing untoward had happened.

It's okay to jump to conclusions in this job. He was eighty-two, so probably not on the list of entrants for the Leeds half-marathon. And when you consider the human body is just a collection of different meats, each performing its own little job, it's no wonder that one day one or more of them will wear out and pack in. You can allow information like that to colour your decision on whether a death like this is just a regular 'sudden' death, or the more noteworthy 'suspicious' variety. But you'd better not let information like that blinker your mind to other possibilities – that's just asking for trouble.

When I've quartered the room – that is, photographed it from each corner to get the most features in each shot – I like to detail anything odd or pertinent. For me, pertinent might include drugs paraphernalia or empty bottles of booze – not that there was anything like that in Albert's bedroom, of course. And odd for me might mean collections of knives or guns, or porn, or an extensive china thimble collection – you get the idea.

Albert could indeed have been the vicar and this house his vicarage; it was, so far, refreshingly free of all such human garbage. His room was that of a man who'd spent serious time in the military, clean and spartan. So, given his age, one might conclude that organ failure was to blame for his death. Only the post mortem could give you that answer, but for now I had to make sure there were no obvious signs of foul play.

I squatted by his thin body, unbuttoned his cardigan and pulled it aside. I unbuttoned his checked shirt and pulled that aside also. Then I pulled up his vest.

He wasn't going to fucking die of hypothermia, wasn't our Albert!

I did this because I wanted to check the abdomen and chest for wounds consistent with beating, stabbing, or shooting. Yes, it sounds crazy – he's an old guy, found dead on his floor – but it's not. I've seen this happen before, where the victim gets carted off to the mortuary because the CSI or the Inspector in charge of the body has deemed it a natural death, and it's almost time to clock off. They release the scene and the next day at the post mortem someone's found a sock rammed down the old man's throat, or they've found stab wounds in his back. It's happened. But it's never happened to me.

His ribs stuck out like someone had laid a white sheet over a toast rack. Anyway, there were no wounds to his chest or abdomen, so I photographed them, pulled the vest back down, and rolled him over, pulled up his clothing so I could see his back. Hypostasis had coloured his white skin a mottled purplish red, so he'd been here in this position the whole time since he died. That made me happy; another couple of photos, and another box ticked.

The Lock

The blood and mucus that had dribbled from his mouth and nose had made a butterfly on the faded multi-coloured lino. That was the last piece of creative art Albert would ever produce. As I was thinking it was better than some of the other modern rubbish I'd seen, I noticed that his right sock was pulled down to expose his ankle bone. Strange. And just as strange were the red smears on his ankle, as though he'd had a really bad itch and had been scratching at the bugger all day long. The top layers of skin had rolled away from the bone like a carpet.

Just one more thing to do on the body, and that was to check his hands and wrists for defensive wounds. I didn't expect to find any, and I was right. But it always amazes me how the skin starts to become translucent in the extremities with the tiny dead veins showing through like rivers on a satellite map. What I did find in his right hand was a key. The dirty fingers were curled around it tightly, a crow's foot of sharp-nailed talons that proved difficult to pry open.

It was a strange key. I turned it this way and that in my gloved hands, wondering what kind of lock this thing would fit.

The Lock

I glanced at my watch, but I really didn't need to; my angry stomach told me it was time for dinner – about one o'clock. I peered out of Albert's bedroom window and saw the officer standing by the gate also checking his watch. He was bored and he was hungry – could probably do with a drink and a piss in equal measure too.

Everyone was waiting on the body snatchers to arrive. I could have left then, having done my bit, but I think it's discourteous not to officially hand over and say 'CSI has completed, it's all yours', rather than having them assume we'd finished and just take a body. That really would be snatching. Wouldn't it?

I turned away from the window and went to inspect the other rooms up here while I waited. I found the bathroom and locked the door while I made use of the facilities. I wondered what lock that key fitted. It looked old and pitted, but it also seemed well-used, no rust on it. And it was an iron key, so it should have rusted as sure as the leaves on the trees outside were rusting. I love autumn.

I checked the other bedrooms while I was up here, aware that the carer was worried about Albert's brother, Frederick. Part of me expected to find a fucking skeleton in one of the beds. I didn't; just empty rooms.

Back in Albert's bedroom, I took the key from him and looked at it again, sure that the body snatchers wouldn't be much longer.

I was wrong. Another half an hour and the bastards still hadn't shown up. I'd tried that key in every one of the grand old doors up here and it didn't fit any of them – not even close. The rooms weren't locked, I just wanted to see what kind of lock that key would fit. And it also added a bit of mystery to this whole thing: I needed to find the only door in this place that *was* locked. Where was Albert going when he keeled over?

I lifted my camera kit onto my shoulder and hurried down the stairs. I decided to throw my gear in the van and then come back inside and continue trying locks with this old key until the snatchers finally arrived and I could go eat.

The fresh air smelled great and even the prickly wind that had rolled in from behind the house couldn't diminish the clear, cool beauty of autumn. I waved at the copper. He waved in return and shouted, "I'm off inside for a pee!"

"Nice," I shouted as I unlocked my van door. "Anything more than three shakes is a wank, okay?"

He laughed and made a dash for the house, shouting, "Been looking forward to this."

I had no idea what he meant, but I suspected needing a pee for a few hours could make someone think like that. I put my camera on the shelf, opened the cab and grabbed my smokes, locked the van door and walked around the corner and back to the house, lighting a cigarette on my way. I didn't much appreciate the body snatchers' broken promises, but sometimes you have to roll with what you're dealt. Luckily, I am known throughout West Yorkshire for my laid-back attitude and for my patience, and just casually finished my cigarette before getting on the phone to them; Postlethwaites, they were called. "It's me, Eddie Collins," I said. "Your men were supposed to be here an hour ago. Where the hell are they?"

At first I thought they'd hung up on me, but when I looked at the phone, it was dead. Forgot to charge the stupid thing up again last night. I will never get used to owning and operating one of these things. Seriously, they're only good for reading on, or playing spider solitaire. Fucking useless otherwise – either you can't get a signal, or they run out of juice and die when you need them the most.

Don't know why, but that last thought reminded me of my mother – ran out of juice and died when I needed her the most. Selfish cow.

I miss her every day.

I flicked away the cigarette and walked back inside the house. The scene guard wasn't around, so he'd either nipped upstairs to use the toilet, or he'd gone back out while I was around the corner at my van and I'd missed him. I listened, heard nothing.

And then I remembered the key in my pocket, took it out and looked it over once more. *Must fit somewhere.*

A cold feeling skittered up my back. It wasn't cold here in the hallway. The skittering was an alarm. It prodded me in the ribs and said that I couldn't legally go snooping around someone's house. Even if that someone was dead.

I am a Crime Scene Investigator. I had ascertained that there was a dead fella upstairs; I'd found no forced entry to the house; I'd found that nothing appeared to be missing, no signs of burglary or theft. I knew he didn't really do the modern thing of collecting more electrical devices than you could shake a shitty stick at, but still, you can tell when some old guy's house has been screwed over, and this place hadn't.

So I knew all this stuff. In short: there had been no crime committed, and the only reason I was there was to record Mr Albert Crabtree's body.

I'd done my job.

I was being courteous in waiting around for the body snatchers, but I had no right to go snooping.

I went snooping. I couldn't resist.

And the reasons I couldn't resist were twofold. I'm nosey, that was the first; and who could resist snooping in a big old house like this one when there was no one around to stop you taking the piss out of the décor or the ornaments? But the second reason I held that key out in front of me and tried to find a door to fit it in, was the noise.

The Lock

The Door

Imagine you were on the third floor of a tower block, and you looked out through the window to see men digging in the road below. Maybe you could see one of them with a sledgehammer whacking some huge stone that was lying half-submerged in the ten-foot by six-foot hole they'd spent the morning digging. That was the noise I heard now.

It was a faint noise, and it sounded distant. Not a tap-tap-tap, but a muted thud-thud-thud. I licked my lips, gripped the key tighter in my hand and set off looking for the door and the lock that it would open.

I almost laughed at myself. I mean, here I was, snooping though some dead guy's house, and I was shitting myself. Of all the scary things I'd done during my career, this one didn't even hit the top fifty. But it reminded me of the countless horror flicks I'd seen over the years – the ones you promise not to get suckered by just as a door bangs or a girl screams and you spill your coffee.

All the same, I felt my heart kick up a notch, and I found myself licking my dry lips. My fingertips were a little damp. It was creepy as hell – but funny, too. I wondered when the first ghoul would jump out at me and shout Oooohoooo.

I covered the ground floor hallway with the torch turned off. I did that so that it wouldn't ruin my night vision, but mostly I did it because I wanted a cheap thrill. I heard a nervous laugh trip and fall out of my mouth unbidden. But still I didn't turn on the torch. I was enjoying the anticipation, I was enjoying scaring myself a little – come on, I had no other stimuli in my life, allow me a little childish excitement.

I slowed as I approached the stairs. I could see them fading into the near-darkness the further up I looked. I saw the newel post, and I saw the hall carpet disappearing into the furthest part of the hallway where the cellar door must be.

I paused by the newel post, wiped my hands down my trousers. I played with the idea of going back outside for another cigarette. I also thought of calling out. I found myself smiling a little, and edged forward again. It would happen any second now: someone would jump out on me, or a rat would scurry over my foot, or the bats would fly into me. I felt myself prickle all over as I waited. I held my breath, creeping one slow silent foot in front of the other. When the knocking came again I almost shat myself.

Thud, thud, thud. My eyes widened, and I could feel the blood rush out from my arms and legs to congregate in my torso where it seemed to shiver as it peered out through my navel.

I was in competition with myself. How much longer could I stand the fear of not knowing before I either ran down the hall screaming like a schoolgirl, or turned on the torch and sent those demons and bats flying off into the shadows, chased by modern LED technology? The torch kept me safe against my silly superstitions.

At the end of the hall I could make out the black line of a doorframe. That must be the cellar door, I told myself.

Behind me, the front door rattled in its own frame, and I squealed a bit. There, I admit it; I squealed. It was only the wind, and I had no doubt at all that it was pissing it down outside. I licked my lips again and thought about just waiting in my van for the body snatchers. Knowing my luck, though, it would start thundering and lightning. I'm kidding; I enjoy a good storm. No, really, I do.

What the hell was wrong with me?

Where the hell were they? Why is patience a virtue? Why can't hurrying the fuck up be a virtue? When they finally showed up, I was going to mash them into the wall.

I reached inside my jacket pocket for my cigarettes and then thought better of it. It wouldn't look professional if I was standing there smoking when they finally arrived, and it would be disrespectful too – this was some old guy's house, and he was dead ... well, it wasn't a nice thing to do. So I decided to go and have a cigarette under the porch; I'd just open the front door a little and light up.

As I began walking, the door handle on the cellar door turned. The door opened with a low-pitched groan that developed into a creak. Of course I'd stopped walking by this point and was trying to see behind me without actually turning to look; my eyes were somewhere at the side of my head, trying to drag my body around so they could do their job.

I was having none of it. Whatever just appeared behind me didn't exist until it touched me on the shoulder. For now, I aimed at the front door to keep my appointment with my old mate, Nick O'Teen.

"Hey, Eddie."

I damned near shat my pants. Again.

I stood rigidly on the spot, eyes so wide that a soft pat on the back would have seen them pop out of their sockets and land on the floor. My breathing hitched and then stopped altogether. My cigarette packet fell out of my hand.

"Where's the toilet? I'm bursting here."

My breath shuddered out in one long groan-sigh. "You bastard!" I said, turning to face the copper who'd gone to relieve himself about twenty minutes ago.

"What?" he said, palms out.

"What? You nearly gave me a fucking heart attack, you prick, that's what."

And he laughed at me, and I almost punched him in the throat. It didn't stop him laughing, though, and I have to admit that once I'd recovered a little bit, I could see the funny side. In fact, if I'd pulled that prank on someone – and it wasn't a prank, he really did need the toilet – I would have laughed my tits off.

I nodded, smiling. "Good one," I said, grudgingly. "Where the hell have you been?"

"Looking for the toilet! And snooping; I've walked past this house for years and always wondered what it was like on the inside."

"You lead an exciting life."

"So where is it? I'm going to piss myself in a minute."

I felt my eyebrows rise. I almost gave a fuck; it scared the shit out of me. "Up the stairs, Hercule," I said. He almost ran up them, and now I saw that the door he'd come out of was the kitchen, and not the cellar head at all. Where the hell was it, then? No way could you have a house this old and this big and not have a cellar. Where else would the staff congregate if there was no old kitchen? Where else would they have the coal delivered?

And then it all got kind of serious.

I heard the banging again. Slower this time, more laboured. I wondered if it was some mechanical device making that sound, or maybe the plumbing, or expansion or contraction? My brain was guessing – but my gut told me that nothing mechanical would make such an irregular staccato noise. I turned on my torch, fed up of playing silly buggers with myself, and found the light switch. Eventually one or two beams of light fell out of the dusty old bulb hanging from the ceiling some eight hundred feet above me.

Seriously, I'd have been better striking a match. Or lighting a fart.

I turned off the torch and put it away. It was amazing how dark it had become, and how quickly. And with the darkness, a new coldness. Wow, this really was turning into a new version of *Scream*, except not quite so funny. The hairs on my neck stood up, and just that subconscious acknowledgement of fear made me angry. Sometimes when I get angry, I get sarcastic too – I know that's really not like me, but on this occasion I allowed myself the pleasure.

I took a deep breath and cursed the fact that my guardian angel was a drunken twat who never protected me from situations like this, when I spotted a key hanging all by itself on the wall. I mean right in the middle of the wall. This wall was thirty feet long, maybe more, and there it was, dangling like it was the last green bottle standing on the wall, waving at me. Now I'd seen it, I couldn't unsee it. How did I not see it before?

I took it from the nail. It was just a regular mortice key, but I looked at it as though it meant I could automatically find the answer to all of life's troubles, and also the door. But that didn't happen either. Christ's sake, I was starting to think this place didn't even have a cellar. Part of me was also starting to think I was crazy for giving a sideways shit in the first place.

Footsteps on the stairs behind me signified either Albert was feeling better, or the copper had managed to go for a pee and survived.

"Body removers not here yet, then?"

I closed my eyes. I want to like people, really I do, but sometimes they're just so fucking stupid.

"I see you found the cellar door."

I opened my eyes as he took the key from my hand and inserted it into a key-shaped hole in the wall beneath the stairs. I was standing four feet from it. Four bastard feet. I blinked like he'd just slapped me.

In my defence, it didn't exactly shout 'door'. It wasn't a door as such. It was in disguise. I mean, there wasn't a break in the pattern of the wallpaper, and below the dado rail or whatever they called it, there wasn't a break in the wood panelling either. There was just a keyhole, not even a fucking doorknob, okay? But he'd spotted it while he was still wondering if he'd spelled his name right in the toilet bowl.

"I want to go home."

He looked at me with a dumb smile on his face, and pushed the door open. Today, I was destined to be outsmarted by a key, a wall, and a man who looked happy because he remembered to zip up afterwards. It was going to be a long day. Actually, it already was.

He was about to say something when he was interrupted by the *thud-thud-thud* sound again. I had to know what the hell was going in this place. Without that sound, I would have been back at the office by now, making up rude names for my boss that only I could understand.

"What the hell is that?"

I shrugged. "Probably a mad axeman."

I could see his entire body stiffen. He wasn't smiling when he asked, "Really?"

"What? No, not fucking really, you pleb." I looked at him, and I asked myself the same question. I whispered, "I have no idea. Shall we go and find out?"

"Do we have to?"

"Come on," I said, "it'll be fun."

The Lock

The Dark

The door closed all by itself. Behind us.

It sent a prickle down my spine that I was too arrogant to acknowledge. It was something we would have to deal with when we had finished our search and returned here.

If I'd been watching this on the TV, I would have thrown a brick through the screen. We were halfway down the stone steps when the lightbulb blew. What were the chances of that happening? This was turning into a badly directed horror show. We both screamed a little bit – him more than me. Much more, actually.

He stopped behind me, and I said, "Don't worry. Just because the light has gone out, doesn't mean anything's changed. There's still a few steps in front of us, and a floor at the bottom, okay? Let's get down there, and I'll put my torch on."

I could sense him nodding, and he whimpered, "Yes, yes, okay."

I didn't fancy fumbling in my pockets for my torch, not with him standing behind me ready to twitch me down the remaining stairs.

"Maybe the noise is just machinery or something," he said. There was only a short pause before he said, "I think we should gather our stuff, and bail out. Really, I've got better things to be doing than checking out a leaking pipe or whatever down in some dead man's cellar."

It was a valid point. But like an inverse threat, I can't have people throw me a dare and not take them up on it. And saying that we should walk away was a dare – no other way of looking at it. "It'll take five minutes," I said. "Come on." I probably sounded quite brave. I'd just been given the opportunity to turn around and pretend I was only getting the hell away from here as fast as my van could carry me because I was busy, and I'd refused the offer. I wouldn't even have lost face. But I'd still refused.

Why?

Because I am a nosey bastard. And at the foot of those steps was the answer to a question that had bugged me for the better part of an hour. Once I was satisfied that it was just a mechanical noise or a mad axeman, I could leave with my chin high.

Oh, and I'm also a bit stupid. The guy who owned the cellar might indeed be dead, but what if the water pipe had burst? What if there was some damage happening right now down there that I could prevent from getting worse? It was the right thing to do – dead owner or not.

We went on into the darkness, me scraping my jacket along the mucky whitewashed walls that – as far as I remember – were streaked with black and dusty spiders' webs.

You know when you think there's one more step and there isn't? It really hurts when the ground comes at you prematurely. I stopped myself falling, and growled at the pain in my left knee. I also issued a warning to Mr Razor Sharp so he wouldn't land on me. And as we both grunted in the darkness at the foot of the cellar steps, we felt the temperature drop considerably as I grappled with the torch in my pocket.

When I shone the light at the ceiling, I could see the fear on his face. I made a quick reassessment of his earlier inverse threat because I hadn't considered his own reasons for wanting out. I decided he could handle it, Christ!

"You okay?" I asked.

He nodded. "Let's just find the source. I have things I need to do."

Yeah, course you do. "Ten minutes," I said.

"You said five minutes. And that was about five minutes ago."

I shone the beam around a room that most closely resembled a phone box without the phone. It was about four feet square, the steps rising behind ... I nodded at him. "What's your name?"

"John," he said. "John Scattergood."

"Course it is. I could've guessed that. Why couldn't you be called something interesting like Ludvik or Igor?"

"What? You sound disappointed."

"Never mind. John." *Predictable bastard.*

"And you're Eddie Collins, right?"

I toyed with denying it. "Right," I said. I hate the fame being a shouty CSI brings to me. I should learn to blend in like all the other wallflowers in my office. I still don't understand them – not one of them gets angry, ever. How can that be possible in a job like this? I'm getting angry now just thinking about it.

I felt a prickle up my back again. He was going to talk to me again, I just knew it. *Time to head him off at the pass.* "Sssshhhh. Let's keep our ears open for that noise again, huh?"

"Yeah, yeah. Good idea."

Of course it is.

So anyway, I shone the torch around our lift-sized box, with the stairs disappearing up behind Ludvik, and nothing but wires and pipes across two more walls, with long-legged spindly spiders running for cover. They made me shudder. The fourth wall had a plain wooden door. It looked well-used. It was black with oily and dirty finger marks all down its opening edge. Shiny with muck.

Thud. Thud. Thud.

We looked at each other. Ludvik licked his lips in determined preparation, like a cracking of knuckles, only quieter. It didn't sound like anything mechanical now we were a lot closer. It came again, and there was no regularity to it. It was thud, thud. Thud. I took a breath and opened that door. Predictably, the hinges squealed. I sighed.

The torch light pushed away the blackness along a narrow dark hallway. What kind of fucking place was this? I'd expected a large open room, with Victorian sinks down one wall, and meat hooks in the ceiling beams, maybe a rack of copper pans still hanging from a rail, I don't know. This was a cold, damp rat run with wires and webs overhead, with uneven, well-worn flagstones, and more brickwork, not painted this time, on either side that seemed to compress you the further in you dared travel. It was a claustrophobic's nightmare.

We walked slowly, backs bent. Grit crunching underfoot and gasping breaths punctuated the silence until *thud, thud, thud* came again and blew our brains out. I swallowed, and stopped at the first door on the right. We waited there as though expecting the thudding to come again and tell us we were in the right vicinity, but typically, it didn't oblige. I handed Ludvik the torch and took the cast iron key from my pocket.

It didn't fit. Nowhere near.

He gave me back the torch and we shuffled along the ever-narrowing passage to the next door. Of course, the key wouldn't fit this lock either. It was the rule of three, and since this whole experience had been like a bad horror movie right from the off, I just walked straight past it. The door and the lock were webbed up anyhow; no one had been through there in decades.

The third door didn't arrive as expected. There was nothing, just more wall. And a few shelves dripping debris-laden webs into their own darkness. The shelves had old tins of paint on them, and brushes with rusting collars and rotting handles. But at their ends, I could see a black seam. And wait, the edge of this piece of wall was peeling. I tapped it, right above one of the shelves. And it was made of wood – painted to look like the wall around it, complete with shelves. Very clever.

And then I looked down at the floor, and noticed scratches in the flagstones. And noticed that most of the debris had been kicked to the sides nearest to the walls, leaving a cleaner path right up the middle. Why hadn't I checked this first?

"Found it," I whispered, triumphant. The triumph was masking a new kind of fear that needled my neck, like having a thistle rolled up and down the skin. I should have declared that I couldn't find the door, and turned right around and headed back out into the rain. Stupid man.

Someone had gone to a lot of effort to conceal a door that led further into a cellar. Why would someone do that?

"I don't like this, Eddie."

"It'll be okay." I didn't know it would be okay. It's just something a fool says to make himself sound wise. And I didn't fancy going in there alone. "I bet it's just some arsehole sitting in the middle of the floor shouting, thud, thud, thud."

Here, the ceiling was a foot lower, the pipes and wires more intrusive; my back bent more. The salt and the mortar from the walls crunched and became slippery on a floor that shone as if wet. It grew even cooler. The smell changed from damp to decay. I wondered if the lightning was sparking off the towers outside, and whether the nearby church clock was fast approaching midnight.

Part of me wanted Ludvik to insist it was a waste of time and that we should be going now. That part of me would've agreed wholeheartedly this time, and beaten the crap out of him to get to the stairs first. But he didn't offer again, and I was far too brave to suggest it. I swallowed, and felt my hand shake as the key slid into the lock.

I looked at him. He nodded.

I turned the key and the lock clicked.

The Lock

The Room

As the door swung inwards, a waft of something like Eau de l'Abbatoir filled my nostrils. There might have been a tinge of mint there too – perhaps a lonely air freshener dangling from a nail in a rafter.

It was at this point that I remembered those old films where the lead man always calls for backup and waits patiently for it to arrive before descending into the bowels of hell, not even tempted into rescuing the damsel and being the hero. It was also at this point that I cursed my ineptitude. I looked at the radio hooked onto my belt. It showed a steady red LED. That told me there was no signal down here. None at all.

Well, there wouldn't be, would there?

"Everything okay?" said Ludvik.

I jumped. "Why wouldn't it be?" *Of course everything was okay; everything was just fine. Prick!*

I managed to assuage my feelings of inadequacy at not calling for backup before descending into the bowels of hell. I did that by telling myself two things. One: I was entering someone's cellar. It was something I had done literally hundreds of times before. And every single time, I had emerged completely unscathed. And two: I *had* backup!

Good ol' Ludvik, remember? He had my back. I was in no danger at all. I suddenly felt much better. I licked my parched lips.

I find it amazing how much bollocks you can tell yourself when you're feeling a bit on edge, and strangely how much of it you're inclined to believe. I actually believed none of it, though. Ludvik? Jesus, come on.

I flicked on the torch again. I felt my heart lurch slightly and then kick up a gear as I ducked and entered the room. It was cold in here. I looked around; it was maybe thirty feet wide and the torchlight died into a vignette before its beam reached the end of the room. And even though at first glance it seemed there was almost nothing in here, it somehow felt cluttered. I felt claustrophobic. I felt on edge. If Ludvik had said 'boo', I would have promptly shit my pants and collapsed of a heart attack – I know I would.

Strangely, the room felt crowded with people, even though I knew there was only myself and Ludvik.

"What the hell is this place?" he asked, looking at me as though I had the fucking answer.

I looked at the door and the lock, saw how substantial they were. They were really meaty, thick and strong, and they'd been chosen to keep people out, I thought.

Or perhaps to keep people in.

Yes, what the hell was this place? I was asking the same question as I took a few strides into the room. The ceiling had the same network of pipes and wires as elsewhere in the cellar. Despite the lightbulbs hanging from exposed fittings screwed to the naked laths every five yards or so, it was as dingy as any cellar I'd ever been in.

I listened carefully and, sure enough, I could hear water dripping. Most of the walls were dry and salty, but there were huge stretches of bricks that were soaked and growing mould. In one corner there was a fungus the size of a dinner plate just hanging on to the wall. You could have used it for your potted cactus and still have room for the picture of the Queen.

Up here by the door, the walls had clearly been painted white many years ago. Now they were blackened in places, especially up in the corners, by thick, dusty webs that draped lazily across them. Every now and then

I thought I saw movement in the webs, but it could have been a trick of the so-called light.

I moved into the room, and felt colder already; I felt damp, too. The floor was shiny under the torchlight, damp in places, and wet with puddles in others. I could almost see my breath clouding before me. I shuddered again.

From here, still just inside the doorway, I could see two grates, and a wire-meshed gulley between them. It was a drainage system. I wondered why you'd need that kind of drainage in an old cellar; what the hell was there to drain? Surely it didn't get that damp?

But if I thought this old cellar was strange now, I was about to look at it in a whole new way. On the ceiling, scattered amid the dusty bulbs, were hooks – large, substantial hooks. The kind of hooks you might see in a butcher's shop. The kind of hooks you might see a side of beef suspended from. Definitely not the kind of hooks you'd find in a Victorian kitchen.

"Eddie?"

Just his voice made me jump again, but its quality added a little extra sharpness to my nerves. "What?

Don't you dare tell me you have to go to the toilet. Just fucking don't."

He had a torch too, except, pleasingly, his spat out a tiny orange glow instead of the huge striking white that mine did. He was pointing to a spot on the wall, six or seven yards from the door.

"Switch," he whispered.

I flicked my torch light at it and, sure enough, there was a small panel of switches roughly where the blocked-up door had been in the corridor. "Go on," I said, expecting nothing to happen. But something did happen. All the bulbs blazed a cruel halogen light that made my torch light look as insignificant as Ludvik's had done a moment ago. They all buzzed, and now the place felt oddly industrial. I turned my torch off and gazed around me, awestruck by what I saw.

PART TWO

Mr Albert Crabtree

My brother and I have lived in this house all our lives. We're into our 80s now, and we were born here. Our parents died forty years ago, and we've lived here together ever since. Bachelors. Both of us. Well, he married once ... but she died in the sixties, during childbirth – her and the baby. We didn't want all that noise and that bother in our lives.

Nobody ever asked. She had no family to speak of, and we always kept ourselves to ourselves anyway. People would call, but we'd get rid of them quickly enough. We were happy that there were no awkward questions after she ... left.

We were also happy to note that dispensing with her gave us both a thrill, and we discovered that all those stupid bra-burning hippy women were right. Placenta was delicious.

We got to thinking that if we could do it to her, we could do it to anyone.

And we knew where to dispose of them, too – in the cellar. We weren't sexual deviants, if that's what you were thinking – we just liked killing people. It was a very enjoyable pastime. Therapeutic, even.

I think it was the anticipation that we enjoyed the most – the begging, the struggling, the screaming. We found that nothing could give us the buzz that this could. And we even practised a silent way to kill people. We used ground hemlock. We fed it to our 'guests', or we crushed it and used its juices in strongly flavoured drinks to render them helpless. The best bit about the hemlock death is the paralysis. They're still conscious until the heart stops, and they can feel everything you're doing to them – you can see it in their eyes. Wonderful. And we also enjoyed the aftermath too – seeing if we'd got away with it. Of course, we did get away with it. We were very good at what we did, and we were very good at lying about it too.

My brother died.

But before he did, we had a falling out. He'd become bored of it. I know how irrational that sounds – every new person brings something fresh that we've never experienced before. A new way of pleading, a new purity in their pleading, a new offer: money, sex, slavery, even. But he didn't see the different nuances in those offers the way I did – I still found it enthralling, whereas he just saw it as begging. He'd taken a dislike to the clean-up as well. Granted, it was laborious, and because of it, we'd slowed down our operation over recent years.

Eventually, it reached the point I'd been fearing for a while. He wanted to stop altogether, and he wanted me to stop too. I think his health was suffering, but anyway, he wanted me to quit and I didn't want to – I still enjoyed it too much. I could have understood it if he wanted out, and allowed me to carry on. But he wanted me to stop too. That just wasn't fair.

I had a decision to make: stop killing strangers, or kill my brother - or at least incapacitate him. I couldn't allow him his freedom, I knew, because there really was nothing worse than an ex-smoker.

No, I didn't trust him.

I didn't want to kill him – he was my brother! So I decided to keep him in the cellar. He knew as well as I did that no one would ever find him. He came quietly, and I locked him in a small room. It had light, and a bed, and a toilet, and its own water tank; everything he needed. He knew he'd be eating burgers as well as bacon and egg – humans taste great in a patty with some ketchup.

When he finally passed, I knew the game was up and it was an end to my fun. Everyone in the neighbourhood knew there were two brothers who lived in the old vicarage. So when he died, I had to report it because even I was growing too old to keep this going for much longer. I still got a great deal of enjoyment from killing, but grinding them up and disposing of them was tedious and stressful, not to mention hard work. It played havoc with my arthritis.

Finding 'guests' was becoming ever more difficult. These days, I couldn't travel too far, couldn't easily overpower them. I had to resort to bribery; money was never a problem, nor was it ever an interest of ours. When you've been gifted everything your whole life, money becomes an irrelevance, it becomes something only the lower classes worry about – silly to think that way, I know.

I also used my deportment, of course. People would think I was an easy target on account of my age and my limp, and they'd plan to rob me as soon as I got them back to my house. This method of capture – the honeypot, I think it's called – seemed rather fitting to me, since it was their avarice that would end up killing them.

The more I thought about it, the more I knew that, at some time or another, someone would discover what we'd done in the cellar. And knowing my luck, even at my age I'd live to see out twenty years inside a cell, and I didn't fancy that very much. So I had to work out how to shift the blame for all that death and depravity onto my 'evil' dead brother. And when I did, they'd label me a victim too ... and take good care of me as my own body fell into decline.

Of course, everyone who visited our Playground discovered what went on in there, but not one of them ever got away to tell the tale. One person, however, finally discovered our secret, and was mesmerised by it. Bliss!

It began eight months ago. I contacted the council and arranged for home help. Frederick was in the cellar by then. He could have screamed when she came by to cook my meal and do a little bit of cleaning – maybe she would have heard him and raised the alarm. But he didn't scream. He knew the carer would end up in the cellar and then she'd go through the bone crusher, and he'd be back to square one. I'd have to beat him, of course. Couldn't let treachery like that go unpunished, could I?

So, Mrs Watkins did three days a week for me for eight months. She also did for an ex-pathologist, so she said, but who knows? Anyway, she always asked where my brother was, and I always shrugged and said I had no idea. I never told her I had a brother, I didn't speak to her very much at all – she was there to wipe my backside and cook for me, and to throw a duster around the living quarters, not to chat. But it showed me that the locals knew there were two brothers who lived at the old vicarage.

Anyway, since I wasn't much of a conversationalist, she never really pressed the point, and eventually she gave up asking altogether. She went through the house snooping while I dozed or read the papers, and that was to be expected, but I was safe in the knowledge that she would never find her way into the cellar. Not that part of the cellar, anyway – we'd made a fine job of disguising it. Even tradesmen who came to fix things over the years never found it.

I suppose I could have done things differently.

We still got mail for him. We still got polling cards for him. Even the authorities knew that two people lived here. We could have arranged for him to have 'moved out', get the authorities to take his name off the house, but he was co-owner, he was on the deeds, and I didn't need all that interaction with solicitors and such. This was a much better idea, and it would ensure I stayed free when all this was discovered – for eventually it would be discovered, one way or another.

When he finally died, I hauled him upstairs into my old bedroom and left him there in the same position I had found him. That was the last time I'd see him, or my room. That day was the end of all my fun. I hated it. But it had to be: we had to swap places, and I had to be good from now on.

I took his wire spectacles, and left a key with him.

You could get through the cellar head door with the normal key that we kept hanging in the hall. Once you were down the stairs, you really needed to know where you were going, or be very inquisitive indeed, in order to find the door into the Playground. And now you'd have to prise the key from a dead man's hand, too.

I had a spare one with me, of course – very well hidden – just in case no one was quite inquisitive enough to find and release me. I didn't intend staying in that cell for longer than absolutely necessary; horrid place.

Once in the Playground, you needed another key to access Frederick's cell. You needed to know where that key was, of course – hanging on a hook inside the door. I had a spare key for the cell with me too. Of course both doors were locked – whoever found me had to believe I had been locked in here for years and left to die.

I remember Frederick banging on the door each time I brought home someone new. He said he'd changed his mind and he wanted to play too, but he was lying. He was lying because he wanted to get out of his cell. But I wasn't taking any chances. I didn't open that door from the day I shoved him in to the day I dragged him out.

I had to convince myself that my name was Frederick and that I was the victim in all this; that my brother, Albert, was a mass murderer and I was trapped here, listening, as he dismembered and slaughtered countless people. Of course it had a bad effect on me. I could feel my hands shaking.

The Lock

I'd been inside Frederick's cell for almost two hours before I heard a bang. The front door. Mrs Watkins was here.

PART THREE

The Cyclone

Ludvik nudged me, "Look, Eddie," he said.

Now that my eyes had become accustomed to the brightness of the room, I noticed that some of the walls and ceiling had been coated with rigid white plastic sheets. Streaks of rust speared towards the floor from screws positioned at regular intervals, and the lower streaks gathered on the greasy floor in pools of orange. Those plastic sheets corresponded with where the saw table was.

Ludvik was nodding towards a framework in the centre of the room, and curiosity pulled me towards it. It was a homemade box-frame about seven feet long with a series of straps anchored along one side of the frame, and a corresponding series of buckles across at the other side. The framework stood about three feet from the floor, and was centrally pivoted at each end so it could be rotated. I stared in horror. It almost looked as though someone ...

My eyes drifted downwards to the floor. I saw redness embedded in the sandstone flags and in the dirt between them.

The floor sloped towards a grate beneath the table as it would in a mortuary.

I bent, and ran my fingers over one of the straps: there was blood ingrained into the stitching and the fabric of the strap, more blood in the buckle. I stood up and looked across at Ludvik. His mouth was open and the fear on his face sent a shudder down my spine. He was standing beside a machine that looked like a wood chipper.

"What the fuck is that?" I asked.

He swallowed. "It looks like this is where … the bones …"

"What?" I walked towards him, eager to find out for myself, because he was making no sense. I looked at the hopper on the top, and I looked at the bucket at the bottom, and all the stuff in between didn't really matter. This was a Turner Cyclone 3000. The enamelled name plate, above a small Union Jack and the proud words, 'Made in Great Britain' declared. But that didn't matter, either; what mattered was the residue in the bucket. It was a white mush, tainted red. It was … "Crushed bone. This is either a DIY butcher's shop," I said, "or it's a fucking torture chamber, Ludvik."

"What?" he said.

"Crushed bone."

"What did you call me?"

"John," I snapped. "I mean, John."

"Why would you call me Ludvik?" He had a smile on his face, but it was an unsure smile, just a little play on his facial muscles as they worked to hide the pain I'd caused him.

"Lighten up," I said, "I was having a laugh, okay? I've just found a bucket of bone mush and you're wound up because—"

"I don't like Ludvik. Why would you have a laugh at my expense?"

Sometimes when I'm a bit stressed, I can let a little giggle slip out by mistake. Well, I full-on laughed at him. "What the fuck are you talking about? Get a grip; I'm not laughing *at* you," I lied.

He nodded, looked away, and mumbled, "Sorry. I just thought …"

We were both stretched by this place, that's all. We were stressed, we were taut with anxiety. We needed to get out of here. "Look," I said, lying again, "I'm sorry about your name, okay. But this is clearly a crime scene, and we need to get the fuck out of here and get the circus involved, okay?"

"Yes," he whispered, "we do."

I took out my phone and wasn't in the least shocked to find it was still dead. I consoled myself with the fact that even if it had a full charge, I'd have no fucking signal anyway. "Your phone," I said, holding out my hand, "does it have any signal?"

He shook his head. "No. I already looked."

I let the last dregs of humour slide off my face. I swear I heard them hit the floor with a splat. No way did he take his phone out. "What about your police tablet? Does that have a signal?"

He shook his head, and though he was staring at the floor, he brought his eyes up to me so that he was gazing at me through the tops of them. It sent me cold. I was only a degree or two away from running for the door, when he smiled at me – a real, friendly smile. And then he began laughing. And then he arched his back and gave out a full-on belly laugh, pointing a finger at me, and trying to speak through the laughter. "Your fucking face," he howled. "Ahaha, you should've seen ..."

"Oh very funny," I said, my heart still defecating on its own little toilet stapled to the inside of my spine. But it *was* funny, and maybe when I'd calmed down in a year or two I would look back on this and laugh like he was laughing now. "Very good," I said again, nodding "That actually was a good one. You had me fooled then. Big time, Igor."

Thud. Thud. Thud.

That stopped him laughing.

We both turned together but the acoustics prevented us getting a fix on the source of the noise. While I was trying to locate it, I spotted another doorway in the corner of the room.

We looked at each other, Igor and I, and I wondered if this might be a good time to exit stage left and get someone down here who wasn't as shit-scared as me. I began walking towards the door we'd come in through, and discovered that it had closed and latched all by itself. If I hadn't been so scared, I would have laughed until I fell over.

"Where are you going?" Igor said, still recovering from his laughing bout.

I pointed at the door. "Nowhere, by the looks of it."

His face became serious, and he hurried to the door. There was no handle on it. "Where's the key?"

I shrugged. "In the lock."

"On the other side of the door?"

I nodded, ashamed. "Sorry."

I watched his jaw clench and unclench, the muscles in his cheeks working hard.

"Never mind that now. Let's see what was making that noise."

I followed him across the room towards the new door, noticing a subtle change in the distribution of power. That cock-up of mine had cost me dearly: Igor was now a level or two above me, and it was as though I owed him. That pissed me off more than being locked in some fucking torture chamber with him. I followed with my tail between my legs.

The closer I got to the door, the more I marvelled at how much darker it seemed here now that there was no plaster on the ceiling above us, just bare laths with blackness between them. The nearer I got to that door, the worse the smell became. It was the antithesis of bleach. It was a rancid human stench. "It's the toilet," I said. "You know, even dungeon masters need to pee."

"I think you should take this a bit more seriously, Eddie."

I nodded, further belittled. Demeaned, even.

This door was solid, like the closed entrance door. It didn't look much like the door to a toilet; not much like an interior door at all, in fact. Interior doors are flimsy, they're there to prevent someone accidentally entering while you're in the middle of your ablutions. They're not meant to shield you from a nuclear attack. This one could.

Igor grabbed the door knob and twisted. It was locked. He rattled the door in its frame but – funnily enough – it was still locked. Set into the wall at waist height was a hole with a serving hatch cut into it. There were remnants of food on the ledge, rings of tea or coffee, milk stains. It looked like one of those hatches you see in cell doors: it had a thumb lock. I wondered if this was where they stored their victims until it was time to …

"Kill them."

"What?" Igor turned and looked at me.

"Thinking aloud," I said. "We need to know if there's anyone in there."

"You don't say." He cocked his head. "Hello. Is there anybody in there?" He folded his arms and smiled at me.

Now he was beginning to piss me off. I could grasp the power concept and how I'd managed to fuck things up royally on one level, but I wasn't prepared to tolerate him imposing it on me every two minutes. I was getting angry, and I was getting hot, and I didn't appreciate the Pink Floyd piss-take either – how did he know I liked Pink Floyd? I fronted up to him. I stared at him, and he stared at me. We must have looked like a couple of boxers psyching each other out before a fight. And trust me, if it carried on like this, there would be a fight.

Eventually, he nodded and backed away a pace or two.

That was enough to break the tension, and I also took a step back; like a handshake without hands, respect given and received. I opened the serving hatch and someone reached out and grabbed my arm. My heart puked its guts up. I screamed and pulled my hand back so quickly that I smacked the back of my wrist on the square edge of the hatch. To his credit, Igor screamed too and leapt a full two yards away.

The top layers of skin on my wrist had rolled up like a carpet and left a trail of tiny red spots as blood leaked out of the capillaries.

"Help me, boy."

I stood there, gawping. The pain in my wrist just an aching memory, and I found myself holding my breath as I stared at him like a loon, my mouth hanging open.

He had watery blue eyes, damp around the sagging red lids. His face was creased, with skin that had stretched and thinned as age had slowly rubbed impending death into each pore. White whiskers bristled his chin and a few coloured his top lip, a counter to the rampant white eyebrows and ear hair. He was almost bald. Wire rimmed spectacles hung off the end of his nose.

He reached out a stick-thin arm to me, and I could see the pleading in his old eyes. "Help. Get me out of here." The dampness around his eyes turned wetter, threatening to spill over. His lip quivered, and I could see his pride melting as his crooked and blackened teeth bit his lower lip to keep it steady . He gasped and a string of saliva whipped across his thin blue lips. Creases furrowed his forehead, and he looked between us. Imploring.

We stood there in shock for a moment. I took my shoulder to the door and all I succeeded in doing was almost breaking my arm. I rubbed it, panting.

"Stop!"

He said nothing else, just pointed behind me at the wall where the light-switches were.

"A fucking key," Igor smiled, dangling it between finger and thumb.

I turned back to the old guy. "Who put you in here?"

Before he could answer, Igor was back with the key. He unlocked the door and opened it. The old man's face crumpled up into something that looked like a punched pillow, and he began to cry in earnest. I had tears in my eyes too as we pushed the door fully open, and entered his den. It was a very sobering moment.

He was struggling to breathe because he couldn't keep his crying under control, and he couldn't keep his crying under control because he could at last walk out of here and embrace his freedom. I briefly wondered what season had been the backdrop to his last outing before he was locked away like this. It was inhuman, and I felt anger that he should have been treated so appallingly.

In the corner of his cell was a wooden lid – something like a top hat – over what I assumed was a hole leading directly into the cesspit, or the sewer from the main room. Nearby was a corner shelf with a toilet roll and some denture cleaner on it. Next to it was an old rocking chair with a crocheted blanket crumpled up on it. And then there was a mattress of sorts, lifted off the bare floor by a couple of pallets pushed end to end and partly obscured by a scattered pile of rancid blankets.

The flagstone floor was partly covered with a grubby linoleum mat, and next to the serving hatch were three or four plates that looked as though they had been licked clean. A tap on a grey wall-mounted tank dripped water into a tin cup on the floor. On the small table by the rocking chair was another tin cup, almost empty.

My heart went out to the poor man. Much as I dislike people, and much as I really dislike touching them – or them me – I felt compelled to wrap my arms around him. I could feel him shivering. I could feel his bones poking out of thin skin. I could smell him. And by God, he stank. "How long have you been here?"

The old eyes squeezed out tears again, and his head creaked around to stare at me. "Years." He gave a weak shrug, and all I could think was that I'd never been so horrified in my life by what one human being can do to another.

Of course I'd seen the aftermath of such behaviour on hundreds of occasions, but I'd never witnessed it ante-mortem before. It made me sick.

"When was the last time he came and fed you?"

"No daylight down here," he whispered. "No idea."

Of course he had no idea, Eddie, you stupid bastard.

Igor held up the metal cup full of water for him. He sipped it gratefully and I pulled myself away from him.

The water spilled down his cheeks and dripped from the tip of his chin to splash onto the floor.

I watched it. And I watched how it landed. And I saw the shape on the floor almost instantly. A butterfly. Red. Like blood. I stared at him, another new fear crawling its way up my throat, clawing at my eyes. I turned and watched Igor, who was still watching him drink, hand out ready to receive the empty metal cup and refill it. I looked at him, trying to study his eyes, but his head was at the wrong angle.

When he eventually did look down at me, I knew that he didn't suspect the old guy of anything. I tried to get his attention, I nudged him, but when he looked, he only smiled, and when he saw I was trying to communicate with my eyes, the way people do when they want to leave a party discreetly, he only looked at me with even more confusion on his face.

He didn't know. He couldn't see. He didn't know about the butterfly shape in blood under Albert's face on the bedroom floor.

And then, as I stood and tried to take a pace or two back from the old man, something struck me in the face like a truck. I remembered Albert's skin, how pale it was – how fucking *white* it was. And yet here in front of me was a man who'd allegedly been deprived of daylight for years, yet he had a better tan than David Hasselhoff.

His hands weren't filthy like Albert's, his nails not as long or as mucky. His skin was cleaner, his whiskers recently trimmed.

But the butterfly was the clincher.

I remembered Albert's ankles, and how the outer layers of skin had rolled up like mine had on the wrist. Albert had been dragged up the stone steps, and his skin had rolled back like a carpet. The wound was post mortem. No capillaries bleeding. In my haste to leave his den, I almost tripped over his blankets.

"What's your name?" I asked, staggering about until a combination of Igor and the doorframe managed to steady me.

I was less than six feet from a serial killer. That knowledge turned my mouth dry. There was something in the old man's gaze, how firmly it held mine, how friendly his eyes were; a kind of resignation in them that said he fucking knew that I knew. I'd been in the same room as him for less than five minutes, and already I'd sussed him out. All his planning, whatever that amounted to, was blown to pieces. Wasted. And I could see how much he hated me because of it.

But still he played along with the charade; perhaps I was reading too much into those eyes. Or perhaps he wasn't afraid of being discovered.

"Frederick," he croaked, and took another sip of water. "My name is Frederick Crabtree. I own this place. Me and my brother, Albert."

I flicked a look at Igor, but he was just gazing at the old man like he was a war hero. "Ah," I said, suddenly feeling very sad. "I have some ..."

Igor put his hand on the old guy's shoulder. "Albert is dead, Frederick. I'm really sorry—"

"No!" the old man screamed.

He did it with such ferocity that it made me shudder. Tears welled and fell and his whole body rocked back and forth. He took off his spectacles and placed his bony hands over his sobbing face. And it was real. If that wasn't genuine grief, he not only had a better tan than David Hasselhoff, he was a better actor too.

That wouldn't be difficult.

Was I wrong? Was there any chance I'd messed this up? Igor was holding him, completely taken in by it all. He looked close to tears.

I'm not wrong. I know what I saw. I bit my bottom lip and looked again at the butterfly. But it was gone; the dripping water and the old guy's movement had smudged it into oblivion.

But look how healthy he is. Perhaps my gauge was incorrect: perhaps I was judging him based upon his dead brother. His dead brother, who might not have taken good care of himself at all, might have rebuffed the carer's attempts to bathe him. Stranger things happened. All I knew was that this man's grief was real.

I went back out into the main cellar to gather my thoughts and take a breath. I wanted a cigarette so badly, but … fuck it. I took the packet out, wandered off up the cellar and smoked one quickly until it burned my fingers.

They obviously thought they'd done a great job of cleaning the walls and the floor, but they hadn't been thorough. I could throw a swab anywhere in this room and get human DNA. I could see smears of blood everywhere I looked. I turned back to watch Igor standing next to the old man. I gritted my teeth.

Yes, I was sure. There was no doubt about it. The old guy in that den wasn't Frederick. They had swapped places.

I'd lay my next month's salary on it. Not much of a wager, admittedly. He was Albert. Maybe he'd kept his brother down here for years as he continued to use this place as a torture chamber. I wondered how much Frederick had witnessed from inside his den. How long this had gone on for? Had Frederick really been locked up in that den for decades ... or had he been a willing participant?

If that were the case, why would his brother turn against him and lock him in isolation? A fall-out, perhaps? Had Frederick threatened to confess? It didn't matter, really; what did matter was that Albert over there had dragged his dead brother up the stairs and tried to swap identities with him. And it was quite clear that the den had been Frederick's home for a period of time, probably until he died.

Then Albert, wanting to escape justice after years of owning and operating a torture chamber without a licence, just blamed his dead brother, and took his identity.

And how do we prove who's who?

If either of the old guys had any useable fingerprints it would be a miracle – from what I'd seen, their fingertips were smooth, so even if either of them were on record, we wouldn't be able to use them. DNA would only be good if one or both of them were on the database, and I bet they weren't.

If I looked at their passports – if they even had passports – I probably wouldn't be able to tell one from another anyway. And then I remembered the dead guy's dentures creeping out his mouth, and in the cell over there was a tube of denture cleaner. A quick visit to the dentist would tell us for sure who was who.

But when it boiled down to it, Albert there could call himself Cynthia Suckface and it would mean shit-all. The only thing that meant anything was: who had performed the torture? Who had killed them, all those innocent victims, and fed them into the Turner Cyclone 3000 bone crusher? My money was on him. Albert. His eyes said so.

I watched the crying old man in the den, and the big cumbersome copper trying to comfort him, and I knew that he'd walk free of all charges. None of the things I'd seen – the whiteness, the rolled up skin, the bloody butterfly – constituted proof. I folded my arms. I had only one thing in my favour.

Bluff.

If Albert hadn't thought it through as I had, if he'd frightened himself into performing in this charade, then he might be frightened into an admission. And for that admission to work, I needed Igor on side to witness it all. I wouldn't need to go into everything with him – not here. I just needed him to understand that something here was very wrong, and that the old guy would have to go into a dry cell as soon as possible after the inevitable hospital assessment.

I walked to the den, and they both looked up at me. I smiled. They didn't.

I wondered how the hell I was going to put the old man at the controls of the bone crusher if he had no fingerprints. How was I going to prove he'd operated that machinery? Perhaps there were some rubber gloves he used, or a facemask; anything that might have his DNA. I would get him.

"Ig— Er, John? Have you got a moment?" I nodded him out of the den and he joined me by the strap frame.

The Floor

As soon as the words were out of my stupid mouth, I knew I'd made a big mistake. "He's not Frederick. He's faking—"

His punch knocked me to the floor and almost knocked my jaw out of my fucking face. I crawled towards the door, knowing full well it was locked, and I left behind a small trail of blood dripping from my split lip. He then kicked me in the ribs and I'm pretty sure at least two snapped. I curled into a ball, and he let me have another couple of kicks before the old man called out.

"John. They're here." He nodded to the ceiling. "The body removers. Go on."

I didn't open my eyes as John hauled me up and dragged me towards the strap table. I was full of aches everywhere and the sharp pains inside my head stopped me thinking altogether clearly as he buckled my wrists up tight. I did open my eyes to see him pull the cast iron key from a pocket and open the door into the corridor. Twat had taken the key out before the door closed – and he'd blamed it on me! The change of power had been all inside my head.

As my eyes closed, they caught sight of him leaving through the door. It slammed shut, and I heard the key turn. And then there was a silence. I swivelled my head around to face Albert. He was already glaring at me. He took off the spectacles and tossed them aside; part of a charade he no longer needed to enact.

"Just you and me now, boy." His smile was cruel. "Curiosity killed the cat."

I managed to stand upright, grimacing at the pain in my ribs. I swallowed. How the hell was I going to talk my way out of this one?

"I'd hoped you, or someone, would find me. And quickly." He nodded towards the den. "It's not terribly nice in there. Everything smells disgusting, and if it doesn't smell disgusting, it tastes disgusting."

"I can't—"

"What I hadn't counted on," he pointed a crooked finger towards me, "was you interpreting things correctly. That was disappointing ..." His voice trailed away and he looked into the distance as though regretting something, or mourning it. "I wanted to start afresh. Indeed, I had conditioned myself to beginning anew." And that's when he looked directly at me, and his eyes made me shiver. "But it seems it was only a temporary abstinence."

The old fucker!

"What's the deal with him?" I nodded after Igor.

"John Scattergood," he said, heading for the den. The further from me he hobbled, the louder his crunching old voice boomed. "He's been coming here for about a year. Helping me out with … with things."

My eyes nearly fell out of my head. It was the obvious conclusion, but to have it confirmed was like another kick in the ribs – and I couldn't afford many more of those. I tried to remain calm – go hyper and I could bet my last breath the old man would join me, and he'd get a real buzz from chopping me into little tiny Eddie bits. Keep calm, however, and there was a chance I could engage him in conversation, maybe find a way out of here. It was a long shot, but it was the only shot I was going to get. "How does it work? He gets to kill one and then you do? What?"

The old man was inside the den, but he soon reappeared. "Something like that. He was good company when Frederick pulled out, but we don't work together, if you see what I mean. I like to perform alone."

"You kept Frederick in there for, what? A couple of years?"

"A year at the most." Albert's eyebrows lifted. "Made of strong stuff, us Crabtrees." He grinned at me, yellow teeth in a disarrayed shambles. "And now," he said, "I wonder what you're made of."

My eyes slid shut, and my guts turned into a Slush Puppie machine. "How many? How many have you killed?"

"Me?" He shrugged. "I honestly don't know. Maybe forty. Maybe eighty. I was never very good at keeping records. Frederick would've been able to tell you; he had an amazing memory. I don't care much for statistics."

He came nearer. And then he walked past me. I twisted around, enduring the pain so I could keep an eye on him. He disappeared into the farthest corner, and then came back dragging a stainless steel trolley.

My heart almost popped. It might have been kinder for me if it had. My legs turned weak, and I could feel them trembling against the material of my trousers. I pulled at the tethers around my wrists, but he'd tied them well, and all I did was rattle the framework and twist my broken ribs.

I heard him laugh as he approached.

I snapped my head around, watching him. He brought the trolley to a halt and stood back, arms folded, allowing me to get a good view of all the tools laid out on the top. It looked like a medieval physician's toolkit crossed with a medieval torturer's playset. Hammers, knives, saws, pointed things, pliers, pincers, and things with screw threads that looked as though they might widen holes …

He stood there and scratched his head. Then the missing thought struck him and he pointed to the ceiling. "Drills!"

I still tried to play it cool, but I knew he'd seen me licking my lips nervously; he'd seen my fingers trying to work at the buckles. I gulped. "This is your last chance to not make a really big fucking mess of whatever life you've got left." It might have sounded brave – I even deepened my voice, strengthened it, to make me appear more powerful – but it wasn't fooling him. I suppose if you've killed a hundred people for a giggle, you've heard it all, all the pleading, all the threats. And I guess that's what gave him his thrills; that, and the screaming. What I actually meant, of course, was, 'This is your last chance to not make a really big fucking mess of whatever life *I've* got left.'

"I don't have that long, Eddie. And I don't mind how it ends." He paused, staring at me with more than a little trepidation. "I hope you don't disappoint." He closed his eyes for a long time, breathing hard. He put his hands up to his head as though trying to squeeze a headache out through his ears.

This might come as a shock, but I've never really been a people person, and now I fucking knew why. But right now I would happily have my testicles sawn off in exchange for a room full of them.

Some of that might actually come true. And not the room full of people part.

If he got off on pleading and screaming, though, he needn't think I was going to oblige.

Who the fuck are you kidding, Collins? You scream at papercuts!

My legs almost gave out, and I pulled at the straps again. "Albert—"

"I know," he said. "They'll come looking for you. I also know they probably won't find you today, but they might find you tomorrow." He grinned, and then he laughed a a little bit like everyone's favourite uncle, friendly, like he was about to offer me a glass of milk or a slice of apple pie. "By then I won't care."

"Really?" I said. "If that's true, that you won't care, why stop at just me?"

The friendly uncle smile turned ugly, became a killer's smile, and he came up to my face, close, like he was going to kiss me. He studied me like I'd just stepped into his Petri dish.

"John?" I nudged.

His eyes looked away. He took a small step back, thinking about it.

"If you're not bothered—"

"Shut up."

We both heard it. Footsteps outside the door.

John was back.

The Lock – Revisited

Albert disappeared from my view as though a fog had descended. But this fog, thick though it was, had a tube cut right through it, and I could see the door. In fact, I couldn't even see the whole door. All I could see was the lock. All I could see *clearly* was the lock. Pin sharp. My hearing amplified the noise of the key sliding into the hole. It also amplified the booming noise inside my chest, and I could feel the blood throbbing in my temples.

I heard the key scraping past the old levers one after another. And then it began to turn, and the levers lifted against their springs and the deadlock began to slide back. There was a solid thud as the bolt hit the stop. There was a pause.

My heart hammered, my eyes were wide and all I could focus on was that door.

It opened. John walked in, and Albert swung the shovel right into his face. Hard. He didn't stop though; the swing carried it on an arc, like a golf club following through after striking the ball. It didn't stop until it glanced off the wall, sparking like flint.

There was no sound from John. There was only a grunt of exertion from Albert.

John fell forward, landed on his side and rolled onto his back where no doubt blood would be leaking into his throat. His face was smeared red, and his eyes were closed, puffing up already. His nose had torn free and was held on by one shredded piece of red skin. How many fractures laced his skull? Blood flowed from his mouth, bringing a couple of his front teeth with it. They fell and tinkled onto the floor before the blood swamped them. More blood leaked from his ear.

I did that. *I* was responsible for that. I didn't know whether to feel guilty or elated. I held my feelings in check.

I saw John's shiny police boots scrape once, twice, against the concrete. I saw the light on his radio glowing red and I wondered when Albert would do the same to me. I kept quiet as my vision widened. My throat had closed up, and I wondered how long it would be before John couldn't breathe through the blood welling up in his throat, but Albert must have been thinking the same. He tossed the shovel away, knelt by his side and pulled John into something like the recovery position. Once there, more teeth came out with the blood like surfers on a good wave.

Albert stood, panting, hands on hips.

Recovering his breath after a minute, he turned and looked at me.

A wave of coldness rushed at me like an arctic kiss. I had no hope of getting away from here alive. This was it; this was where Eddie Collins, average arsehole, would take his last breath.

He pointed at me. I shuddered. "I'd better put the freezers on," Albert said as he walked past me, holding his stomach.

"You'd better get him an ambulance."

He laughed.

"I mean it. Stop this before it goes too far. Get him some medical attention!"

"It was your idea, Eddie."

Shit.

"So what? I didn't think you were fucking psycho enough to hit him with a bastard shovel!" And then I realised what I'd just said, and to whom. I waited for the footfalls to turn around and come for me, but they didn't.

"We've never needed a doctor down here before, and I won't be breaking that tradition this evening."

He was a walking paradox: he looked ill, like he'd eaten bad food, and yet he was like a younger man already. It was like watching a vampire growing younger after drinking a victim's blood. It seemed he could barely contain his excitement at getting down and dirty again; quashing that illness and relishing the thrill of the kill again.

Pity I'm the kill.

"Bones and meat go through the crusher much better if they're just a wee bit frozen. Don't want them frozen solid," he continued, "otherwise the screw sticks, and the blades go blunt. And they're not cheap." He disappeared into the darkness again, and must have turned a switch I couldn't see. The freezer hummed and the lights dimmed just a little.

He came back into view, dragging his cardigan. He stood before me in a stained white vest, panting again. "Going to get hot," he whispered. His arms were sticks with skin spray-painted over the top, and I had no idea where he'd found the strength to smash John in the face like that.

I stared at him. His eyes didn't move from mine. It was like a battle of wits, a pre-torture test. I looked away, letting him win this round. His eyes were weird: they were hard, made of glass, unfeeling, uncaring, and there was a tick in both lower lids that made him look like a cartoon. He rubbed at his temples again.

I was a spectator across the room, looking at a skinny old man in a vest staring at a coward in a uniform whose wrists were tied to a crazy torture frame. And I was being out-stared by a fucking skeleton.

Hang on. 'Coward'? I don't fucking think so, Collins.

I know, I know. He was my death and he was going to make me suffer before I found it, but come on. Was I going to make it easy for him?

I gave him a hard stare of my own. His own eyes widened slightly, barely perceptible, but I noticed it. I had shocked him; it was tantamount to mutiny.

"You couldn't stop, could you?"

"I beg your pardon?"

"You. You stupid old fucker. You just couldn't resist one more kill, could you?"

"Two more."

"Prick."

"Mind your mouth, boy."

"Fuck you."

He made to back hand me, but I didn't flinch. He wanted me to, he wanted me to cower, and maybe he wanted me to beg. He got nothing.

"You almost had it, too. You almost convinced me that you were Frederick – just another one of Albert's poor victims. But you were too greedy."

He almost smiled. "Carry on talking, Eddic. Mcans nothing to me. I've heard everything over the years. I already told you that. Be as angry or as meek as you wish, be as provocative or as compliant as you will."

I surprised myself by being the one to smile this time. And it was a full-bodied 'up-yours' smile. "I'm going to fucking bury you, old man. I'm going to—"

In an instant he'd dropped the cardigan and slapped me round the face. And then he grabbed me by the throat, fingers digging in, pulling me forward to his own face. He breathed his stench on me and screamed, "You're going to die, boy! That's all you're going to do. And you're going to die well." He pushed me away, laughing. "I'm going to enjoy this one the most."

I went to kick him, but he was blindingly fast and stepped aside with time to spare.

He just wandered off into the shadows again, groaning, leaving me alone to ponder how long I had left. I searched for something to help me. I needed to get my wrists out of these buckles, but there was nothing within reach. I had a multi-tool in a canvas pouch attached to my belt, but I had as much chance of reaching it as I had of ordering a Big Mac and large fries. And of course my phone was dead. Bastard.

I looked across at John. I could see him breathing, but he was almost dead. The front of his skull was breached in so many places that brain damage was inevitable. I wanted to wave an apology, but it seemed flippant. So I turned my head away.

Albert shuffled back to me and I snapped my head around as the whip came into view. He cracked it and before I knew what the hell was going on, the bastard thing had wrapped itself around my legs.

Albert grinned. And then he pulled.

My feet slipped out from under me and I hit the floor, busted ribs first. The pain was white-hot and ripped through me like someone was tearing me in half. I didn't scream. I bit my tongue, though, and the blood flowed down my chin and dripped onto the cracked flagstones. The framework above me rocked from side to side with my weight. Albert pulled my feet around until the straps at its far end were in reach.

He bent to put the strap around my ankle, and I kicked his face. It must have connected well because he bucked away, hands cupping his mouth, and a smear of blood came away on his fingers. He straightened as much as his old man's back would allow, took away his hands, and smiled at me through blood-stained teeth. And then if he didn't fucking laugh at me! Crazy bastard.

"Very good, lad," he said. "I was off my guard. You taught me a good lesson." And then he walked away into the shadows again.

I scrabbled my feet on the floor, trying to push myself upright again, but it was like trying to push a length of rope uphill. I pulled with my wrist tethers but my strength was depleted, and the straps dug in until I couldn't feel my hands anymore. I was more or less horizontal, with my arms pulling out of their sockets. I was shaking, scared shitless of what he was going to come at me with next. I didn't have to wait long.

I heard it before I could see it.

It grated across the floor, and even though I couldn't yet see it, I could guess what it was. It was a sledgehammer, and I could imagine it digging in to the flags, leaving a white trail of crushed sand behind it. It stopped right in front of me. I turned my head away. Sweat ran into my eye and blood choked my throat. I coughed it out, and my ribs punished me for it. I saw him lift the sledgehammer.

"Kick me, would you?"

"Whip me, would you?" I yelled.

He laughed again. "Feisty one, eh? I like them feisty. It really livens things up. I like to try and guess when they'll lose their feistiness. They all do, you know. They all turn into whimpering wrecks before long. Even the big tough men." He raised his eyebrows, stood the hammer upright again, and rubbed his stomach. He bent over, rested his hands on his knees, as though he was going to vomit. The next moment, he was over it, standing up, and grinning at me again.

"I have to say that you're not up there among the best. I'd managed disembowelment before the really tough ones let go. You won't make it that far." He rested his bony elbow on the hammer shaft as he caught his breath. "I just need you to know that once I've broken your legs, I'll be leaving you alone for a bit while I work on him." He pointed across to John. "I'm not about to waste him just because I have you to play with. Waste not, want not.

"I'm going to strip him, and then I'll drag him to the bench. That's where I'll peel him, and turn him into a set of spare ribs and a nice collection of steaks." He watched my eyes.

I fucking shut them. They were battling the pain, trying to keep it away so I could focus.

"Not much point in doing anything else with him. It's like kicking a dead dog. So I'll just cut him up, get him in the freezer for an hour or two. Then he goes through Betty." He stepped closer, and whispered, as though we were the best of friends. "Betty the bone crusher," he said. "She's only got a two-horsepower motor, but she's never let me down." He paused, as though reminiscing.

I opened my eyes again, and looked at madness in human form.

"Frederick reckoned she'd churned out nearly four and a half tons of people." He nodded, pleased with that statistic. "And I only change the blades once a year ... That's good old British engineering for you."

"I thought he was your partner?"

"John? Oh yes, he was. But now he's just another guest."

"But why? How could you do that to someone you know?"

Albert's eyebrows met in the middle. "I don't understand your concern. It doesn't matter to me who he was, I just—"

"But it must matter. You couldn't kill Frederick, could you?"

He pondered on that for a second or two. "No. No, I couldn't. His was a natural death. But I suppose his being family must have counted for something. I hadn't given it any consideration before, so I thank you for making me consider it now." He shrugged, "But John is just ... well, he's no one. As are you, of course."

He stopped talking.

"Do you have any feelings?" I didn't even know why I bothered asking. The answer was plain.

"Which would you rather happen: you get your freedom, or I get arrested? Better still, my death or your freedom?" He walked around me slowly. "You're good at your job," he said. "Anyone can see that. I made errors that you spotted right away. I should have known it was a flawed plan. I bet you're at the top of your tree, Eddie. No one's better, and you know it, too. You're arrogant. You're so arrogant that you cannot comprehend that this is happening to you.

"This kind of thing always happens to someone else, doesn't it? And you're always the hero who comes along and works it all out, makes sure the victim gets justice and the suspect gets locked up. It's very noble," he said. "But this really *is* happening to you, Eddie." He bent over, hands on his knees again, as he studied my face. "And there's no way out. You'll take your last breath here in this room, and I'll be here to see it. Me."

I could tell that he was masking some kind of injury or illness now. The smiles had gone. He had a straight face that couldn't quite hide his anxiety. His body was throwing him a curveball, and he didn't understand why – or why now.

"To see someone's death is something of a privilege. It happens to so few of us that to witness the passing is ... not a delight, as such, but certainly an honour." He coughed again, and this time he bent double, keeping off the floor only courtesy of his fingertips.

But I felt no sorrow for him. I had my own problems to contend with: pain hit me from all corners, and I was beginning to find it hard to concentrate. My hands felt like they were ready to fall off. "Sorry," I said, "could you repeat the question please? I wasn't listening."

His face was almost as white as his brother's. "My death, Eddie – or your freedom?"

"My freedom," I said. "I'm only human, after all." I tried to smile, but it just wasn't fucking happening. "Did you expect me to be honourable and ask for your death? You'll die soon enough anyway."

He said nothing, but his head bowed slowly so that he was left looking at the flagstones and his feet. I saw him shake his head, not disagreeing, but as though he was trying to rid his head of something – the headache, perhaps?

"You know, when this is all over, they'll find you. And they'll try you. And you'll end your days in a cell."

He looked up then, eyes gone watery.

"If you think it'll be easy, you're very wrong. You probably won't make it through the remand process while they check out all those deaths you're responsible for. It'll play havoc with your stress levels. And then the trial will be months long. Every day sitting there, handcuffed, listening to experts, hearing people shouting at you from the public gallery. Your pencil sketch on the news every night. The only variable will be the length of your sentence."

He blinked at me.

"And even that is immaterial: anything over five or six years would just be public appeasement, because you'll die inside pretty quickly. Winters are harsh in a brick cell, and prisoners harsher still."

There was a prickle of fear in his eyes.

I'm winning.

"Now," I whispered over the hum of the freezers, "which would you prefer: your death, or my freedom?"

He knew that if he killed me, there might be less sympathy with his plight as a deranged old man than if he let me go and waited patiently for the police to arrive.

He'd effectively killed John, so I supposed there was nothing to stop him having one last fling and killing me too. But he'd hesitated far too long now for it to be an impulsive killing; he'd stood and given his own future some thought, and that had an effect on his next move.

My heart lurched from one coarse beat to the next. And when Albert finally broke into a smile that should never have existed, I was sure I felt it stop altogether. He'd reached a decision.

"Be right back," he said. "Won't keep you."

I watched him slip back into the shadows, coughing his lungs up now, and leaving the hammer standing there as if waiting for instructions. Of course I wanted my freedom – who wouldn't? – but I also wanted this bastard caught and charged with however many counts of murder he was guilty of. Who knew how many families were out there agonising over a lost loved one? He could give them an answer. I worked on the buckles as I heard him working twenty yards behind me, pulling at some new torture machine or another.

Whatever happened to just breaking my legs?

I pulled at the buckles. The leather straps were an inch and a half wide, and because I couldn't get one hand across to the other, I couldn't remove the buckles myself. All I could do was pull. The straps wouldn't break, but I hoped the rivets holding them to the metal frame might pull out. I pulled and pulled, grimacing against the pain in my ribs and in my arms. The whip was still wrapped around my ankles, and I could feel the pins and needles growing in my feet.

I don't think I've ever been in so much pain without howling about it.

PART FOUR

Mr Frederick Crabtree

I suppose I became tired of it when one of them died before we'd even begun having any real fun with her. I felt cheated. We had lots of cleaning up to do, and we'd had less than two hours with her. Heart failure, I suppose. And frankly, it was days like this when I wondered if it was all worth it. I could be out walking, or sitting in the parlour reading with a glass of gin. Instead it was my turn to cut her up, part freeze her, put her through the bone crusher, and destroy her clothing. A lot of work for very little return.

I was becoming too old for it. I admit it. Oh, of course Albert still relished it. The fun of watching death arrive as one stared into the – Guest's? Entertainment's? – Victim's eyes wasn't something one could easily forget. It truly was a wonderful sight. And many a time we'd discuss whether we could feel the soul leave the body. We could never prove that one way or the other, of course, but it was fascinating for a while.

Anyway, I'd grown tired of watching their eyes. Albert had not. I tried to talk him into a life free of killing – not because of any moral virtues I had suddenly acquired, but because it was becoming tedious. We discussed it, we debated it, and then we argued about it.

He won. He wouldn't hear of it.

He always did win. Albert always got his way; he was a spoilt child, and now he was a spoilt old man. But he was slightly bigger than I, and older too. His superiority inevitably won out.

And – despite giving my word that my abstinence was a choice I had made, and in no way should it be seen as untrustworthy, or treacherous, or treasonable to him in the continuance of his hobby – I could tell that he didn't trust me. Stupid man.

I knew we'd arrive at this impasse.

I remember when my wife was still alive. We all lived here together, and I thought we all got along jolly well, actually. Well, except for our gambling: mine and Albert's, I mean. Barbara had asked that we stop. It was rather expensive and our income had depleted over the previous decade or so, and perhaps it would have been sensible to quit while we were still wealthy.

He wouldn't quit. I always thought this was because the original suggestion had come from Barbara, and not from me – not that he would have stopped if I had suggested it, but I think he would at least have considered it more fully. Because it wasn't my suggestion, though, he flew into something of a rage and went out on a full weekend's gambling spree. Lord knows how much he lost.

I had tried then to reassure him that Barbara wouldn't interfere in our pastime again. He had become quite cross about it all, and he had given me 'that' look one evening. 'That' look always spelled disaster, it seemed.

My brother always could talk me round. I have just discovered – just realised – that killing Barbara was entirely his suggestion, though at the time it seemed like a super idea, and what's more, it seemed like my own. I distinctly remember him clapping me on the back and saying it was a jolly fine idea. He wanted to kill the infant inside her too. The infant was his; I have long had problems in that department, so it couldn't have been mine. He literally killed two birds with one stone: the child, because it was his, and Barbara, because she was crude enough to suggest an end to his social entertainment.

He got his way.

She was just another Guest, after all. In truth, I didn't miss her too much.

But the point is, he got his way with everything in our lives, and so this time, before declaring my intention to stop killing, I tried to work out what he would do about it. I knew he wouldn't trust me to keep my mouth shut – I knew it for a certainty. But I also knew that he wouldn't kill his own brother. I reasoned that he'd have no option but to cage me. And the only place he could do that without too much work would be in the old coal chute and storage place in the cellar, alongside the Playground. I supposed, too, that because of its proximity with the turntable, and the table saw, and the crusher, it would add a little spice to his routine if he knew I was listening and suffering. I was sure he'd factor that into his decision.

Having worked this out, I began making a collection of hemlock as I took my weekend walks through the woodland and the country lanes that ran through it. That small amount of cultivation had been inspired by a book I came across in the library almost a year earlier: *The Lost Art of Poisoning* by Sir Thomas Winstanley. I was fascinated by it. I was also educated by it.

The months passed, and both of our bodies began to fall into a steady decline; mine quicker than his. My outings ceased, of course, but by then it didn't matter – I had everything I needed to take my revenge.

Albert was awarded some lady who called three times a week to clean for him and prepare his food. He kept their meetings short and cold – he couldn't abide company unless it was the disposable kind, and he refused to acknowledge me whenever I came up in conversation. Of course, I didn't receive any such luxury; I was in the cellar, whiling away my time. He would come to me and tell me she'd been asking after me. I think he found it entertaining that someone was asking after me, and he took pleasure in drilling it home that he was afforded care, while I had none.

My body is failing fast in this darkness, and my revenge is close.

My plan is this: upon my death, Albert will remove me from the cellar, take me upstairs and perhaps clean me up a little, and take my spectacles. Then the infernal carer will find me and mistake me for him – we are not dissimilar, though he is slightly larger, and does not wear dentures. She will summon the police and they will declare one Albert Crabtree deceased. But it won't end there. The police will find him locked in the cellar, pretending to be me, Frederick.

He has keys to get him in there and to lock the doors behind him as he proceeds. So long as he hides those keys well enough, he'll be fine. He won't be in there long, anyway; just from the morning of my death until the police find him. He'll make sure not to be in there long – he cannot abide being without his comforts.

He will then go on to tell them how his wicked serial-murdering brother, Albert, kept him a prisoner down here while he killed twenty or so people. (In fact, it was almost one hundred – I have them all written down in my journal – also secreted in the cellar along with my suspicions of Albert's plans.)

I am hiding nothing from them. I shall document the very best part of my plan: the hemlock. There is no running water in there. There is a galvanised tank of sorts bolted to the wall with a tap beneath it. It sits directly above my latrine, which is a hole in the floor above the drainage system we installed for the cellar some twenty-odd years ago. The hole has a grille over it, and it also has a wooden cover to try to keep the smell down. It's where we would rod the drains should they ever become blocked – they never did.

The water in that tank is fed from the kitchen upstairs. He turns on a tap each day for five minutes and voila, my tank is full. Cold water, yes, but full. And I dictate how I use that water: drink it, wash in it, or flush the latrine with it.

My life is almost at an end now. It is time. I have saved some drinking water in a juice bottle, and infused my tank of water with hemlock.

I know, or rather I hope, that when he comes down here, stuck in my pathetic little room, he'll be worried. He'll even be a little frightened. After all, it would take just one very keen-eyed officer to discover the duplicity, and the game would be up. He'll be worried, and he'll get thirsty. I'll make sure that my juice bottle is empty. And he'll partake in a cup or two of my tank water. Perhaps sampling my life by drinking from a galvanised tank will add authenticity to his plight.

The Eyes

He coughed. Really, violently, coughed.

He was behind me. Maybe twenty or thirty feet away; I couldn't really tell because I couldn't crane my neck that far back without getting cramp. And when I'm trussed up like a turkey dinner, cramp is not high on my wish list.

Anyway, why should I care?

I closed my eyes. And I treated myself to pretending I wasn't trussed up – just for a minute or so – and I wondered what I'd do.

Albert was an eighty-odd-year-old fella who was a multiple murderer. He just killed a police officer right in front of me, and will go on to cut the poor bastard up if his health holds out.

But anyway, back to the meeting I was conducting inside my head. If I was free to walk around this dungeon, what would I do about poor old Albert?

As I saw it, there were several options open to me. I could kill him for being a killer. I could take retribution for the four and a half tons of people he'd put through Betty the bone crusher.

"Eddie."

I ignored him and continued my meeting. The second option was to just walk out through that open door there and leave. I could have a cigarette outside in the rain with the thunder and lightning bringing Armageddon all around me. And then I could call CID, get the old prick arrested, and go for something to eat.

Spare ribs, maybe?

Or I could walk out of that door, close it and lock it behind me. I could resume my duties, blaming my absence on a technical issue, or perhaps a bowel issue, and just carry on with the remainder of my day, happy to let the old fucker die slowly and rot down to a powder. All well and good – until the new owner buys the place and wants to turn the cellar into a pool room. Among the blood in the room, the police would find mine. 'Oops,' I'd tell them, 'sorry, forgot to tell you'. And then I'd have to convince them that I didn't kill John and the old geezer. Not ideal.

"Eddie!"

"Shut up! I'm trying to think."

Albert shuffled past me and back towards his den. Considering he was all for having me beheaded five minutes ago, this was something of a surprise. But I was still wondering what to do if I got the chance.

I left the meeting pretty quickly when I heard him come back out of his den. He was breathing heavily, and I could see even from here that his eyes were rimmed red like someone had just pepper-sprayed him. He looked ill, but he also looked determined. I didn't like that look, especially when it was combined with the evil-looking hunting knife in his right hand.

"Aw, come on, Albert," I said. "It's gone too far for this shit. You need medical assistance, you don't need to start cutting me up!"

He brought the knife closer, and I could hear his breath grating down a throat that was obviously constricted. He tried to smile at me, I could tell, because he wanted to scare me, but it didn't scare me – it angered me. I whipped about, but couldn't free my legs or my wrists. "Albert!" I shouted. "I'm warning you."

I had no idea what the hell I was warning him of, but I was trying to break through to him and make him understand how pointless killing me would be. But it wasn't a smile at all; it was the grimace of silently borne pain.

He stood before me, sweat beading on his face and on his arms. He was shaking, and I could see clear snot leaking from his nose. The knife trembled in his hand.

I swallowed.

He brought the knife up and sliced through the straps holding my wrists. I hit the floor like a sack of shit, and because I couldn't even feel my arms, let alone control them to break my fall, I planted the flagstones face first. It hurt. A lot. My lip opened up again and I felt blood running down my chin.

I also landed on my busted ribs, and screamed as the blood returned to my dead arms. Touching them was painful.

Now it was my turn to pant as I stared into the very sharp and very pointed end of that knife. It was literally an inch from my eyeball. It was so close that the nearest thing in focus was a set of liver-spotted knuckles, and I could make out the hairs on his arm as it twitched this way and that.

My eyes soon arced upward towards his face, and once there, they noticed how wide his pupils were, how grey his skin was, and how blue his lips were. If I didn't know better, I'd say Albert was a drug user.

"You have to help me," he said.

His voice was cracking on each syllable, and he had problems forming the edges of the consonants. There was a vile smell seeping from him, and a brown sludge on his chin that could have been blood, but equally could have been vomit. This guy was rotting from the inside out. Quickly. I was forming my first reaction – confusion – when he kindly filled in the details for me.

"He's poisoned me." He retracted the knife, and crabbed away a couple of steps. He almost made it to standing upright before he had to crouch again, hand over his guts, teeth showing a grimace, eyes squeezed shut.

"Poisoned?"

"Hemlock. I knew that water tasted bad. I thought maybe the tank was rotting or something."

"Serves you right," I said. "I can't believe you kept your own brother in there."

He shot me a look of impatience, "I loved my brother!"

"What the fuck would you have done if you weren't so keen on him?"

"Please, Eddie. I need a hospital."

Wow. This was my daydream, like five minutes ago.

Only now it was real. I shook my hands out, removed the whip from around my ankles, hissing at the welts, and pulled myself up. Once I made it to my feet, I found I was sweating. "You need a hospital? Are you having a laugh? You've killed dozens of people in here, probably slowly, enjoying their deaths like they were a matinee at the Odeon ... and you want me to call you an ambulance?"

"Please," he said. "I need a doctor." And then a steely determination grew in his eyes; his mouth, though still twisted with a pain I hoped I'd never know, grew a tinge of a smile. "You're a public servant, Eddie. You have to help me."

"I thought you didn't want a doctor down here creating a precedent." I looked away; I had to. If I'd taken in any more of his smug bastard's face ... I scared myself with thoughts of what I'd actually do to the man. I shuddered at the prospect of becoming a murderer, either directly by physically assaulting him, or indirectly by sitting down and having a smoke while he expired on the floor in front of me.

Can't do that, Collins.

There were two distinct things that prevented me. Firstly, I liked to sleep at night. No amount of booze or sleeping tablets would let me rest if I wilfully took another's life. Fortunately, we have law and order in this country, and I can hand over my problem to it and let it deal with murderers and rapists and leave me with a clear conscience. I don't have to bloody my hands or sully my mind with people like him.

And secondly, I fight for justice every day. What right did I have to take his away? Or to take away the right to justice of any of his victims? None at all. So the next time I walled up some creature for breaking the law and ruining other people's lives, I knew I was doing it to uphold the law, and not to break it for my own satisfaction. I couldn't choose when and how to be judge and jury, could I? That would be two-faced.

Albert grunted at me.

I turned to look at him just as a blur of movement snatched my attention from Albert's eyes to his neck. Two prongs from a garden fork protruded from the front of his neck. At first, his eyes looked at me in surprise, but it didn't take long for that to turn to horror. He clawed at them, slowly at first, and then frantically as bubble-filled blood spewed from his neck and turned his stained off-white vest a dark brown colour.

He took a last attempt at a breath, and when it didn't work, he simply fell forward, his legs remaining rigid. He looked like a tower block being demolished. The worst of it was that he didn't take his eyes from me, as though having someone launch a garden fork through his neck was my fucking fault. He hit the floor on his face, and I saw the fork punch back out of his neck an inch or two as the prongs hit the floor first.

The gap he left in front of me was filled by an equally grotesque sight.

John stood there wobbling. I couldn't believe that he was still alive. I honestly thought that the mess Albert had dragged away was just a lump of meat wrapped in a police uniform.

His face was bloody chaos. I could just make out the reds of his eyes through the slits of his swollen eyelids that shone with blood and tight skin that looked ready to burst. I could see the blood still seeping from his ear, and more that had begun to crust over on his cheek. His hair was matted with sweat, his lips had burst and split vertically so although his mouth was closed, I could still see his teeth quite clearly, and hear the whistle as he sucked in air.

Mostly I could see the tears running from his eyes and turning red as they coursed through the blood on his face. I didn't know if that was because his eyes had suffered some damage and the tear ducts had burst, or if he was actually crying.

He was shaking.

And now the problem called Albert was replaced by a similar problem called John. I still preferred Igor, if I'm honest.

Well, it was the inverse problem.

"Kill me," he mumbled. It came out as 'Ki-ee', but I got the drift.

When the look of horror finally left my face, I nodded my understanding at him. I swallowed, my throat dry and my tongue clacking against the roof of my mouth. "You've no idea how much I wish I could oblige, you worthless piece of shit." I shoved him in the chest and he fell over backwards. A part of me wanted to hear his fractured skull crack against the floor, and watch his brains dribble out of his ear on a tide of blood. And part of me was frightened that I'd hear his fractured skull crack against the floor and see his brains dribble out of his ear on a tide of blood.

Honestly, being so full of contradictions is a bane of mine.

He squirmed in an ever-growing pool of blood.

I knelt by his side, fuelled by my increasing anger. "Life is hard enough for people without having to deal with arseholes like you. You're there to protect us from people like him. You're not there to become him! I can't think of a worse betrayal of trust and office. You fucking scum. I hope you live."

I stood, and bit my lip until it began to bleed again so that my mind would be pulled away from the temptation to kick him in the head as hard as I could. And I walked right past him, and out through the open cellar door with its beautifully ornate cast iron lock and key.

The Thud

When it happened this time, I stood still, completely rigid, and my booming heart hushed while I listened to that 'thud' again. I was sure it was that old noise I'd first heard, the one that had tempted me to come down here hours ago. But I wasn't sure. I held my breath, and it came again, though much quieter this time.

Thud, thud, thud.

I blinked. I turned, and I walked back into hell.

It was unnerving to see John sitting upright, staring at me through slits, with a new kind of fear on his blood-smeared face. He tried to reach out and stop me as I walked by.

The thud came again.

We both jumped. Reluctant feet pushed my shaking body forward, stuttering as though unsure of what they were getting us into. Now it was my turn to walk into the shadows at the back of the dank, inhuman place. I could hear two chest freezers humming. These were the ones Albert had gone to switch on a lifetime ago. But then I saw a third freezer. This one's lights weren't on. This one wasn't plugged in. It had dried blood down the front. It had a padlock hasp screwed into the lid and the front, a rusty nail in place of a padlock. Why on earth would anyone want to put a lock on a freezer? Unless they wanted to stop something getting out.

In the dim light I stood there and stared at it.

It thudded again and I nearly screamed.

I could see my own hand shaking as I reached out and pulled the nail from the hasp. I flicked the hasp up and off the loop. I took a breath, swallowed and then heaved the lid open. A pair of feet pulled back and kicked the side of the freezer. I leaned in slightly, and the first thing I saw was the blood down the front of a white shirt. The second thing I saw was a school insignia on a torn blazer.

He looked up at me. His red eyes squirted tears and he tried to burrow into the floor of the freezer. Poor kid was beyond petrified. His hands were cuffed in front of him, knuckles split and bloody, and he pulled himself in tightly, trying to protect himself. I was horrified that he could think I was part of John Scattergood's circle of killers.

"My name's Eddie Collins," I said, trying to keep it friendly. "You're safe now. No one is going to hurt you, okay?"

I smiled at the kid and wondered what it looked like from his perspective: the silhouette of a man whose face is a sheet of blood, trying to smile but not quite getting it past a sneer, reaching in towards him.

But, to his credit, he let me take a hold of the solid bar of the cuffs, and slowly help him stand. I helped him out of the freezer, and then pulled the cloth away from around his mouth.

"I have to tell you, son, that your handwriting is abysmal."

The End

I reached into my pocket for my cigarettes, and was distraught to find them crushed and soggy.

Despite that, it had never felt so good to be outside in the rain before. By the time I'd stumbled all the way to my van and unlocked it, I was soaked and most of the dried blood had washed off my face to leave open wounds.

Part of the reason I hate my bosses so much is because of all the new technology they push on us. But because of it, once I got back to my van, I had backup, and I had the entire fucking circus in that basement before that piece of shit could die on me.

Author's Note

I write crime thrillers, and have done since 1996, the same time I became a CSI here in Yorkshire. All of my books are set in or around our biggest city of Leeds. I don't write formulaic crime fiction; each one is hand-crafted to give you a flavour of what CSIs encounter in real life. Every book is rich with forensic insight to enhance your enjoyment.

Get in touch.

For more information, or to sign up for my Reader's Club, visit www.andrewbarrett.co.uk. I'd be delighted to hear your comments on Facebook and Twitter. Email me and say hello at andrew@andrewbarrett.co.uk

You can make a big difference.

Did you enjoy this book? I hope you did. Honest reviews of my books help bring them to the attention of other readers. So if you've enjoyed this book I would be very grateful if you could spend just five minutes leaving a short review.

Reader's Club Download Offer

GET TWO **FREE** BEST-SELLERS AND A **FREE** SHORT STORY.

Building a relationship with my readers is one of the best things about writing. I occasionally send newsletters with details of new releases, special offers, and other news.

Sign up to the Reader's Club, www.andrewbarrett.co.uk, and I'll send you all these **free** goodies as a thank you:

A Long Time Dead, the first in the Roger Conniston trilogy.

The Third Rule, the first book in the Eddie Collins series – a 500-page best-seller.

The Lift – a first person short story. Climb inside Eddie's head and see life as he does.

Also by Andrew Barrett

Visit Andrew's website (www.andrewbarrett.co.uk) from where you'll be able to choose your favourite place to buy his books. Why not sign up to the newsletter while you're there, and get more freebies and more news?

THE SOCO ROGER CONNISTON TRILOGY

THE CSI EDDIE COLLINS SERIES

STAND-ALONE THRILLERS

Thanks!

There's a long list of people to thank for helping to pull this book, and all of my books, into something that reads like it was written by someone who knew what they were doing. Among them is my amazing wife, Sarah, who makes sure I get the time to write in the first place. There can't be too many people who accept "I want to think of things" as a valid excuse to avoid life for a while – but it seems to work!

To Kath Middleton, and Alison Birch from re:Written, a huge thank you for making sure the first draft wasn't the final draft – you will always be the first people to read my books, and consequently always the first to point and laugh at my errors. It's because of you that this book has turned out so well, and it's because of me that you had so much work to do to get it there.

Thanks also to my Facebook friends in the UK Crime Book Club, my Andrew Barrett page, and my Exclusive Readers page for their constant encouragement – who knew readers could be so assertive, demanding... and kind.

The Lock

is dedicated to Jean Wigglesworth; a
grandma like no other...

Printed in Poland
by Amazon Fulfillment
Poland Sp. z o.o., Wrocław